MW01143237

Words Around the Year

by Roy Doty
illustrated by
Sal Murdocca

SIMON & SCHUSTER BOOKS FOR YOUNG READERS
Published by Simon & Schuster
New York · London · Toronto · Sydney · Tokyo · Singapore

January
SNOWFLAKES
SNOWPLOW
SNOW-BOARDING
MUFFLER
NO FISHING
SKIER
SKI BOOT
TOBOGGAN
SNOW
SQUIRREL
ICE SKATE
MITTEN
SNOW ANGEL
SLED

SMOKE
ICICLE
SNOW BLOWER
FIRE
MARSHMALLOW
SKATER
ICE
EARMUFFS
POND
SKI POLE
SNOWMAN
SNOWBALL
SNOW SHOVEL
SKIS
BOOT

February

CHIMNEY

BIRD FEEDER

DECK

WEATHER VANE
DART BOARD
BUNK BEDS
CHEST
GARAGE
BASKETBALL
MICROWAVE
LADDER
HOSE
SHOVEL
RAKES
DRYER
WASHER
CAR
STOVE
LAWN MOWER

March
DOG BED
NEW
FANCY CAT
WITH EXTRA VITAMINS
FANCY FISH
SCRATCHING POST
PUPPIES
KITTENS
CAT FOOD
FANCY CAT
FANCY DOG
FISH FOOD
HAPPY FISH
WEASEL
SKUNK
GERBIL
CHAMELEON
TURTLE
SNAKE
LIZARD
IGUANA

BOWL
LEASH
LOVEBIRDS
MYNAH
BONE
TELEPHONE
CASH REGISTER
CLIPPERS
DOG FOOD
COLLAR
DOG
GUINEA PIG
CAGE
PARROT
COCKATOO
CANARY
FISH
FISHBOWL
AQUARIUM
DISH

April
APRIL FUN
BILLBOARD
FIREHOUSE
ENGINE 9
CHURCH
CARPETS
APRIL SALE
STREETLIGHT
HOUSE OF FASHION
DYNASTY GARDEN
SAVINGS BANK
CLOTHING STORE
FIRE FIGHTER
CHINESE CUISINE
FIRE ENGINE
POLICE OFFICER
LEE'S PRODUCE MARKET
HOT DOG VENDOR
FRANKS
CROSSWALK
CANNON
LUNCH DELI GROCERY
HAMMER'S HARDWARE
STORE
STATUE
MAIL TRUCK
MAILBOX
FIRE HYDRANT
TAXI

POST OFFICE
UNITED STATES POST OFFICE
GAS STATION
MOVIE THEATER
COMING SOON!
STAR
TWO SHOWS DAILY
MY TWO CATS
DUMP TRUCK
DELIVERY VAN
CEMENT TRUCK
STOP
STOP SIGN
POLICE CAR
OLD BOOKS
S&N VIDEO
DRUGS
PIZZA
AWNING
PIZZA PARLOR
FOUNTAIN
BUS
STREET
BUS DRIVER
APRIL
BEST PICTURE
MY TWO CATS

May
MOTHER'S DAY FLOWERS
ENTRANCE
SIGN
LILIES
FLOWER BED
DAISIES
DAFFODILS
GLADIOLUS
WATER
STATUE
GARDENER
SPADE
WATER LILIES
PANSIES
ROSES
HEDGE
UMBRELLA
ICE CREAM
ICE-CREAM CART
IVY
THE MAY MAZE

TREE
FISH
SUNFLOWERS
BRIDGE
CROCUSES
FOUNTAIN
SUNDIAL
GERANIUMS
EXIT
SHOVEL
WHEELBARROW
VIOLETS
FOXGLOVE
TULIPS
BENCH
VINE
FLOWERPOT
WALL

June
JUNE
BICYCLE
TIGHTROPE
ZEBRA
CAMEL
GIRAFFE
TUMBLER
BAREBACK RIDER
POLE
HORSE
RINGMASTER
JUGGLER
BEAR
MONKEY
PENGUIN
RING

AERIALIST
TRAPEZE
ROPE
CLOWN
CAGE
UNICYCLE
TIGER
LION TAMER
OSTRICH
CHAIR
LION
ELEPHANT
BALLOONS
DUCK
DOG
CLOWN CAR

July
CROW
COWS
SHEEP
HAYSTACK
LAMB
POND
OWL
ROY'S FRESH FARM
PRODUCE
JULY 4
SALE
ASPARAGUS
SQUASH
RADISHES
BEEHIVE
SCALE
CORN
TOMATOES
CARROTS
CUCUMBERS
CAT
BASKET
MOUSE

WEATHER VANE
N
E
W
S
SCARECROW
SILO
FIELD
PITCHFORK
HAY
TRACTOR
BARN
CHICKEN
RABBIT
PIG
HORSE
TRUCK
DUCK
CORN AND MORE
DOG

August
HAPPY AUGUST
KITE
AIRPLANE
DUNE
VOLLEYBALL
NET
CAMERA
LIFEGUARD
UMBRELLA
SUN HAT
SAND
SUNGLASSES
BOOK
TOWEL
COOLER
BEACH CHAIR
RADIO
SHOVEL
SUNTAN LOTION
PAIL
SEASHELL
CRAB
STARFISH

PELICAN
SEA GULL
LIGHTHOUSE
SAILBOAT
FISHING ROD
PIER
SNORKEL
MASK
SAND CASTLE
BEACH BALL
NET
FLIPPER
FISH

September
TENNIS RACKET
TENNIS BALL
LADDER
SLIDE
RINGS
CLIMBING ROPE
SWING
STROLLER
SCOOTER
POGO STICK
ROLLER SKATES
ROLLERBLADES™
TIRES

FRISBEE™
BICYCLE
HOOP
BASKETBALL
BENCH
WAGON
JUNGLE GYM
UMPIRE
TRICYCLE
BAT
JUMP ROPE
GLOVE
BASEBALL
HOME PLATE

WITCH
OCTOBER
BROOM
CROW
SPIDERWEB
OWL
SPIDER
SCARECROW
FENCE
GHOST
FLASHLIGHT
MAIL DROP
BALLERINA
LETTER
HOBO
RABBIT
CLOWN
BAG
MONSTER
COWBOY
PIRATE
BUCKET

BAT
CHIMNEY
LADDER
JACK-O'-LANTERN
HAUNTED HOUSE
IRON GATE
SKULL
SKELETON
IVY
CHAIN
LOCK
RIP
GRAVESTONE
October
BLACK CAT

November
BALLOON
NOVEMBER
GRANDSTAND
TURKEY
CLOWN
ACROBAT
PRINCESS
MAYOR
UNICYCLE
CASTLE
NATIVE AMERICAN
TRAMPOLINE
KNIGHT
PILGRIM
HORSE
FLOAT
STILT
JUGGLER
COWBOY
NOVEMBER

FLAG
235
CONFETTI
TV CAMERA
SPECTATORS
TUBA
TRUMPET
TROMBONE
DRAGON
MAJORETTES
JESTER
DRUM
SAXOPHONE
DRUM MAJOR
POLICE OFFICER
MOTORCYCLE

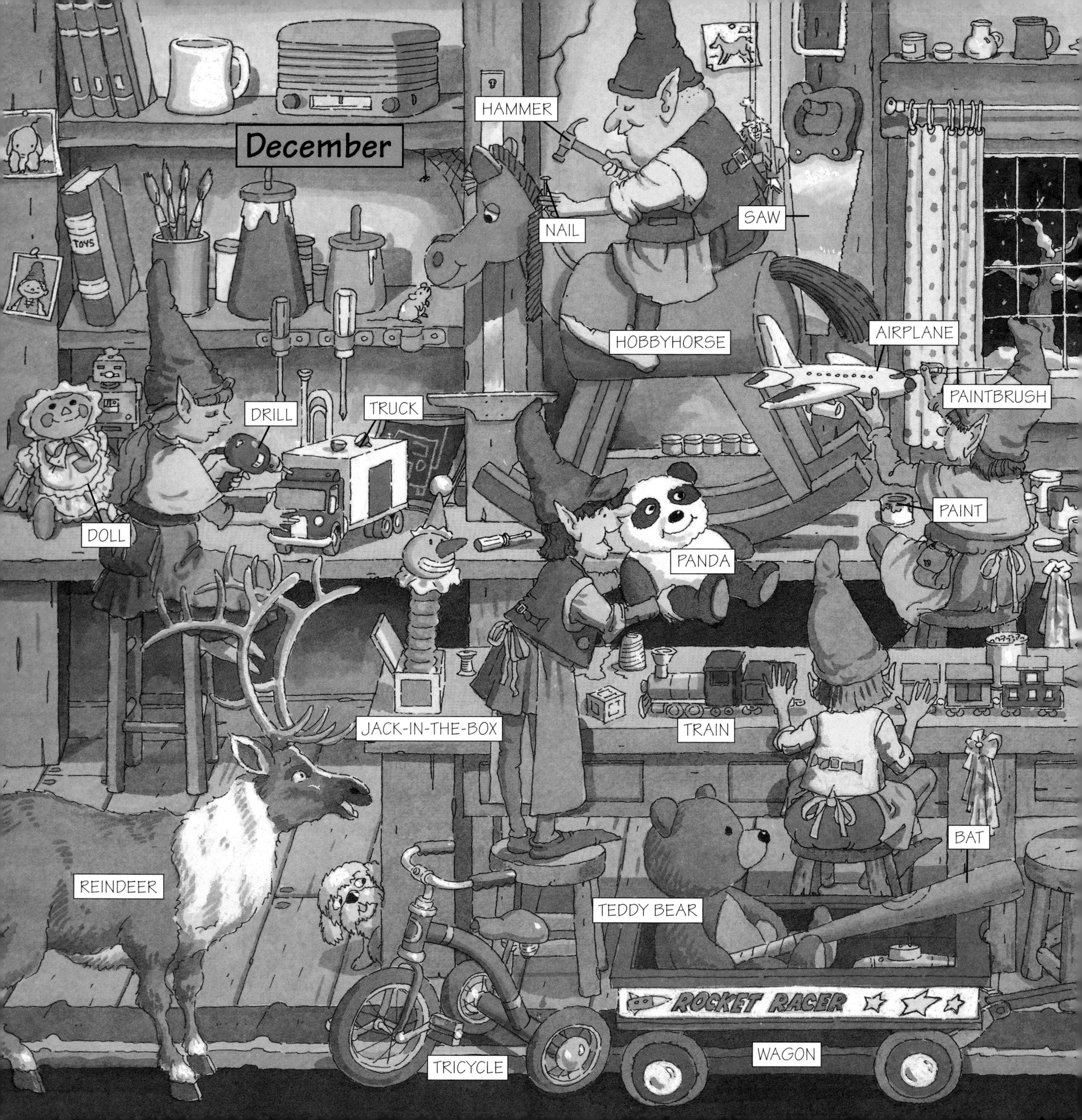
December
HAMMER
NAIL
SAW
HOBBYHORSE
AIRPLANE
PAINTBRUSH
DRILL
TRUCK
DOLL
PAINT
PANDA
JACK-IN-THE-BOX
TRAIN
BAT
REINDEER
TEDDY BEAR
ROCKET RACER
WAGON
TRICYCLE
TOYS

PICTURE
DECEMBER
S M T W TH F S
1 2 3
4 5 6 7 8 9 10
11 12 13 14 15 16 17
18 19 20 21 22 23 24
25 26 27 28 29 30 31
CALENDAR
DOLLHOUSE
SANTA CLAUS
COMPUTER
DESK
CHAIR
BASEBALL MITT
TOY SOLDIER
DRUM
ELF
SCOOTER

To Rachel, the last word in granddaughters
—R.D.

To Nancy
—S.M.

SIMON & SCHUSTER BOOKS FOR YOUNG READERS
Simon & Schuster Building, Rockefeller Center
1230 Avenue of the Americas, New York, New York 10020

The text for this book is set in 12 point Tekton.
The illustrations were done in watercolor.
Manufactured in the United States of America

10 9 8 7 6 5 4 3 2 1

Library of Congress Cataloging-in-Publication Data
Doty, Roy. Words around the year / by Roy Doty ; illustrated
by Sal Murdocca. p. cm. Summary: Labeled illustrations
introduce words associated with each month.
1. Vocabulary—Juvenile literature. 2. Months—Juvenile
literature. [1. Vocabulary. 2. Months.] I. Murdocca,Sal, ill.
II. Title. PE1449.D66 1993 428.1—dc20 92-19312 CIP
ISBN: 0-671-77836-6